Two Little Monkeys

MEM FOX · JILL BARTON

PENGUIN|VIKING

Two little monkeys
playing near a tree,
one named Cheeky,
one named Chee.

Hello, Cheeky!
Hello, Chee!
Better stay close
to that big old tree!

Look out, Cheeky!
Look out, Chee!
Something's prowling—
what could it be?

Two little monkeys
run to a tree,
one named Cheeky,
one named Chee.

Scramble up, Cheeky!
Scramble up, Chee!
Scramble up
that big old tree!

Two little monkeys
tremble in a tree,
one named Cheeky,
one named Chee.

Hide away, Cheeky!
Hide away, Chee!
Make sure you're hidden
in that big old tree!

Two little monkeys
peep from a tree,
one named Cheeky,
one named Chee.

Who **is** that prowling?
What do you see?

Oooooooh....
Scary!

Careful, Cheeky!
Careful, Chee!
Don't fall out
of that big old tree!

Two little monkeys
leap from a tree!
One named Cheeky,
one named Chee.

Well done, Cheeky!
Well done, Chee!
What a brave leap
from that big old tree!

And now you're safe—

as safe can be.

You clever little monkeys,
Cheeky and Chee!

For Cate, with love
—M. F.

For Nat, Soph, and Al, Livi and H.
—J. B.

Mem Fox has written many celebrated picture books, including *Where is the Green Sheep?*, *A Giraffe in the Bath* and the bestselling modern classics *Ten Little Fingers and Ten Little Toes* and *Possum Magic*. She lives in Adelaide, Australia, where she spends heaps of happy time indulging in monkey business with her grandson. Visit her at MemFox.net.

Jill Barton has illustrated numerous award-winning picture books, including *Rattletrap Car* by Phyllis Root and the bestselling *Baby Duck* series by Amy Hest. Jill lives in Devon, England, where, when not drawing or painting, she likes to monkey around with her family and friends.

VIKING
Published by the Penguin Group
Melbourne · London · New York · Toronto · Dublin
New Delhi · Auckland · Johannesburg
Penguin Books Ltd, Registered Offices: 80 Strand, London WC2R 0RL, England
Published by Penguin Group (Australia), 2012
1 3 5 7 9 10 8 6 4 2
Text © Mem Fox, 2012
Illustrations copyright © Jill Barton, 2012
The moral right of the author/illustrator has been asserted. All rights reserved.
Cover and internal design by Sonia Chaghatzbanian
Manufactured in China
National Library of Australia Cataloguing-in-Publication data available.
ISBN 978 0 670 07652 9
puffin.com.au